Little Chimp
Runs Away

Story by Jenny Giles
Illustrations by Rachel Tonkin

Mother Chimp and Little Chimp are going down to the river.

Little Chimp is running.

Little Chimp is running
into the trees.

He is running away.

Mother Chimp

can not see Little Chimp.

"Come back here,

Little Chimp!

Come back here!"

Little Chimp sees a snake
in the grass.

"Oo-oo-oo!
Oo-oo-oo!"

The snake sees Little Chimp.

Little Chimp is running
back to Mother Chimp.

Where is Mother Chimp?

Here comes Mother Chimp.

She can see Little Chimp.

Here comes Little Chimp.

He can see Mother Chimp.

Little Chimp runs
to Mother Chimp.

Little Chimp is going
down to the river
on Mother Chimp's back.